Tree House in a Storm

To Alicia –
Climb high!
Rachelle Burk

by Rachelle Burk

Illustrations by Rex Schneider

Stemmer
House
Publishers

Inquiries should be directed to:
Stemmer House Publishers
P.O. Box 89
4 White Brook Road, Gilsum, NH 03448
www.stemmer.com

Library of Congress Cataloging in Publication Data
Burk, Rachelle.
Tree house in a storm / written by Rachelle Burk;
illustrated by Rex Schneider. — 1st ed.
p.   cm.
Summary: When nine-year-old Kenny's tree house is destroyed by
Hurricane Betsy, he plants an acorn that grows into a tree, and many years later,
his children use it to hold a tree house of their own.
ISBN 978-0-88045-169-7 (paperback)

[1. Tree houses — Fiction.   2. Hurricanes — Fiction.   3. New Orleans (La.) — Fiction.]
I. Schneider, Rex, ill.   II. Title.
PZ7.B9179Tr   2009   [E] — dc22   2009014228

Printed in Canada

To survivors of natural disaster worldwide
~ R.B.

Some people say Kenny was born in a tree. He climbed them as soon as he could walk.

When he was nine, he nailed
scraps of wood to the trunk of
a mossy oak that stood in the
woods behind his house.

His sister Allison helped him drag over old boards, and soon they built their own fort where they ruled as king and queen.

They were sure it was
higher than the tallest
building in New Orleans,
higher than the puffy
summer clouds,

...even higher than the stars of the Milky Way.

It was safe from invasion by grown-ups, because the steps up the trunk were too narrow for grown-up feet. "But we'll have to protect it from monsters," Kenny warned his sister. "Monsters?" Allison shuddered. They took turns with binoculars to guard against an attack.

They spent the muggy summer days amidst the breezy leaves to escape the heat. They sipped lemonade, smacked mosquitoes, and told stories.

Then Mama would call, "Time for lunch!" but even peanut butter and sliced banana sandwiches couldn't lure them down.

So, Mama put the
sandwiches and
bunches of juicy grapes
into a basket between
the gnarly tree roots.
Kenny and Allison
hauled the basket up
by a rope.

Their kingdom was peaceful until one dark September day. That's when the monster attacked. Her name was Betsy.

"Keep your pets indoors," warned the TV newscaster. "Evacuate!" said the radio announcer.

Betsy was a hurricane, and she was meaner than an ogre.

"How can a storm be so bad?" Allison asked Kenny. "Mama always said rain and thunder can't hurt us."

"A hurricane isn't a regular storm," he told her. "It's like a storm having a terrible tantrum."

Mama brought flowerpots and lawn furniture indoors so they wouldn't blow away. Dad boarded up the windows to protect them from breaking when the fierce winds came. Kenny grabbed his tools and scrambled up the old oak tree. He pounded extra nails into creaky, wobbly boards until the tree house was secure. Then he raced back inside.

Soon the wind picked up. It shook the walls and
rattled the windows. The family quickly packed an
overnight bag. They drove to a shelter in the city
where there were cots, warm blankets, and food.

It was a sturdy brick building where people
would be safe until Hurricane Betsy got over her
tantrum and blew away. Wind, rain, and lightning
whipped and flashed like an angry dragon. Hours
seemed like days as strangers talked, played
cards, and prayed through the stormy night.

The next day, the air grew calm and blue skies appeared. Kenny pressed his nose against the window of the station wagon as they headed home. In silence he gazed out at the flooded streets and at trees that had been uprooted and tossed like bowling pins.

Allison gasped as they drove past a wooden home
that had blown down in the night. "Just like in the
Three Little Pigs," she said.

"Where will they go?" Kenny asked. "I don't know," Mama said, her voice cracking. "But people pull together and help each other in times like these."

When they turned onto their street, the family
sighed with relief to find their home had only lost
a few window shutters and roof shingles. Then
Kenny thought about his tree house and bit his lip.

He ran out and sloshed through the muddy woods to the oak tree.

A broken limb dangled in the breeze like a hangman's noose. Huge branches lay on the ground surrounded by mangled wood. All that remained of his fortress were the steps up the trunk. Kenny's kingdom of dreams was nothing more than splintered limbs and jutting nails.

His eyes filled with tears. Mama came over and held him close. "It's okay," Kenny said, wiping his eyes. "We were lucky." He knelt down and plucked the fattest acorn from a fallen branch.

He took it to his yard and buried it in the wet ground. Allison helped him pat the soil. "We'll be all grown up before the tree is big enough to climb," she sighed. Kenny put his arm around her shoulders. "But when it is," he said, "we'll build a great tree house."

Years passed and the acorn grew into
a strong, mossy oak in the middle
of my grandparents' backyard. And
Kenny, my father, grew too.

Together we built this tree
house, higher than the church
steeple in Jackson Square,
higher than the rainbow after
Hurricane Betsy, even higher
than the glowing moon over
the Mississippi River.

During long summer days, my brother and I sit in
our tree house among swaying branches and curious
wrens. We sip lemonade, smack mosquitoes, and
tell stories. At lunchtime Grandma sends up peanut
butter and sliced banana sandwiches.

Dad and Aunt Allison help
us watch out for monsters.
Sometimes Dad gazes across
the yard in silence, as if he sees
his old tree house beyond the
rooftops. It was a lot like this one,
he says, except for one thing . . .

...the steps up the trunk of this tree are wide enough for grown-up feet.

The End

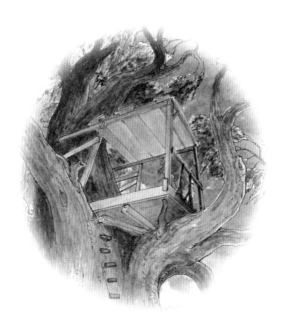

Author's Note

Hurricane Betsy hit New Orleans on September 9, 1965. Many lives were lost, and there was devastation through much of the Gulf Coast. My family lived in a part of the city that sustained minimal damage, and we were able to return home the next day. Although my brother's playhouse was lost in the storm, we felt fortunate that we were safe and our house was spared.

In 2005, my childhood home was swept away by Hurricane Katrina in a tantrum even larger than the earlier storm.

Rachelle Burk juggles careers as a social worker, children's entertainer, freelance writer, and rescue squad volunteer. Her inspiration for *Tree House in a Storm* came from her experiences growing up in New Orleans. She now lives with her husband and daughters in East Brunswick, New Jersey. Visit her online at www.rachelleburk.com

Rex Schneider has illustrated seven books, including *I'm Nobody! Who are You?*, *The Wide-Mouthed Frog*, and most recently *The Art of Moving Picture Posters* from Stemmer House Publishers. He pursues his loves of story telling and gardening from his Blue Mouse Studio in Michigan.